BOB THE BUILDER™

A PRESENT FOR BOB

adapted by
Elizabeth Milton

based on the episode "A Present for Bob" written by Miranda Larson

LITTLE, BROWN & COMPANY
LB kids

Little, Brown and Company

Hachette Book Group
1290 Avenue of the Americas, New York, NY 10104
Visit us at lb-kids.com

LB kids is an imprint of Little, Brown and Company
The LB kids name and logo are trademarks of Hachette Book Group, Inc.

The publisher is not responsible for websites (or their content)
that are not owned by the publisher.

First Edition: October 2016

ISBN 978-0-316-27293-3

10 9 8 7 6 5 4 3 2 1

1010

Printed in China

It was almost time for Christmas! Bob and Wendy were filling up Muck and Scoop's buckets with decorations for the Spring City Christmas display.

"So this is all we need?" Bob asked.

"Yes! Everything else is on site," Wendy told him.

Muck revved his engine with excitement. "Then let's go! I can't wait to start building!"

The team went to the site, but Lofty stayed behind. He wanted to add more twinkly lights and snowflake decorations to Bob's Yard!

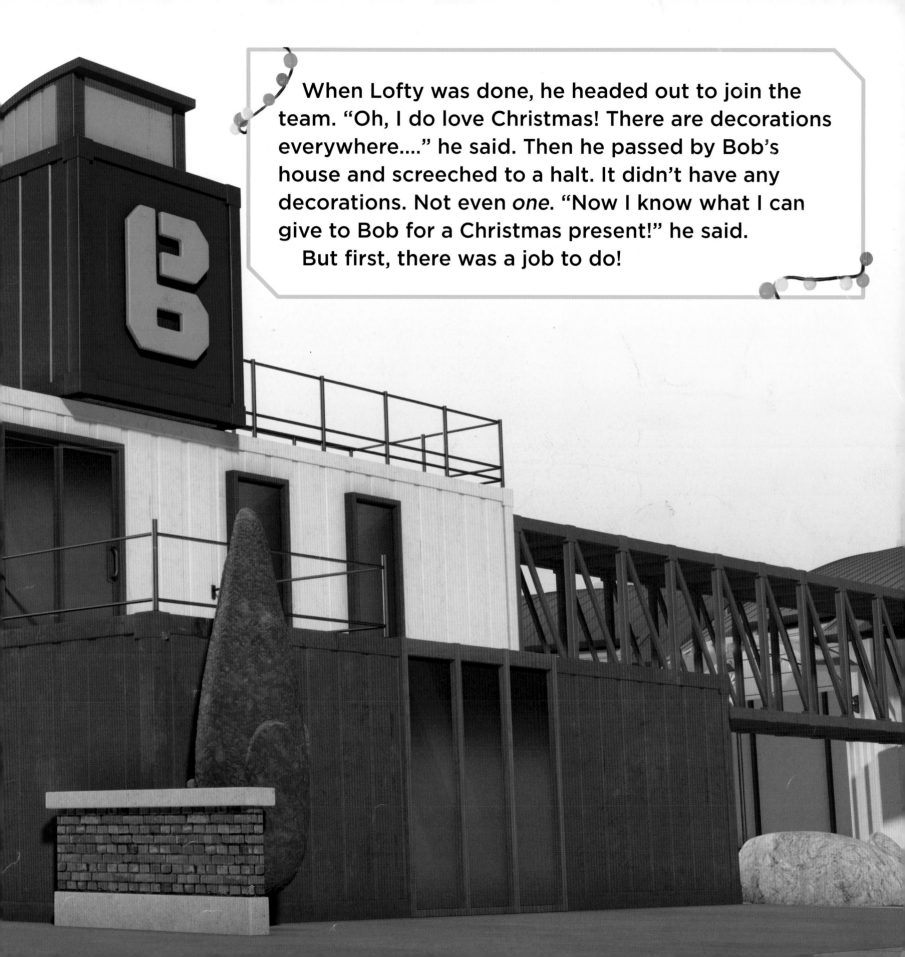

When Lofty was done, he headed out to join the team. "Oh, I do love Christmas! There are decorations everywhere...." he said. Then he passed by Bob's house and screeched to a halt. It didn't have any decorations. Not even *one*. "Now I know what I can give to Bob for a Christmas present!" he said.

But first, there was a job to do!

At Spring City Plaza, everyone got to work. Scoop and Muck unloaded decorations. Bob and Leo prepared the base for the Christmas tree in the center of the plaza.

"Bob, is the base for the tree ready?" asked Wendy.

"Yep!" said Bob. "All we need now is the Christmas tree!"

That is when they heard a familiar sound: *"Beep! Beep!"* It was Two-Tonne! He was hauling a huge tree. "I've got rather a large one here," he said.

Bob was ready to get the job done. "The mayor is switching on the tree lights tonight. So, can we build it?" he asked the team. "**Yes. We. Can!**" they cheered.

Lofty arrived and lifted the tree from Two-Tonne's loader. He carefully lowered it into the base.

Next, Bob, Wendy, and Leo attached three support cables to stop the tree from tipping over.

Finally, Bob and Leo laid out the ice tiles.

The Spring City Rockets watched the action from behind the safety barriers.

"*Ooh!* The floor looks like ice!" Brandon said in awe.

They saw Lofty drive by with a present dangling from his crane hook. "Is that for the display?" asked Saffi.

Lofty smiled. "It's for Bob," he said, "and I can't wait to give it to him!"

First, Lofty needed to help Wendy hang the tree lights. He put the present under the tree to keep it safe.

When Scoop and Muck saw Lofty's present, they didn't know it was for Bob.

"Let's put the other display presents here, too," Scoop suggested.

"Okay, Scoop!" Muck agreed.

Meanwhile, high above the Plaza, Bob and Leo were standing on a support platform. They were setting up snow machines on the side of a skyscraper.

"You said to prepare the snow," Leo told Bob, "but I can't find any!"

Bob smiled. "We're going to make *pretend* snow using a special liquid and these machines!" he explained.

Lofty gasped when the lights came on. "Bob is here and the lights are twinkling," he said. "This is the perfect time to give him his Christmas present!"

When Lofty looked under the tree, he saw lots of display presents, but none looked like his gift for Bob.

"Where could it be?" Lofty wondered. He used his crane arm to move display presents out of the way. It bumped into one of the tree's support cables, but Lofty didn't notice.

Snap! The cable broke in two, but Lofty wasn't paying attention. "There!" Lofty spotted Bob's present! He stretched his crane arm to try to reach it. "Just a little bit farther!"
Snap! Another cable broke.

Lofty tried to move his crane arm again, but it was caught in the tree! He was stuck! "Okay, don't panic!" he said to himself. "Just back away slowly and gently." His wheels skidded on the ice tiles. "New plan. Give one, big...pull!" Lofty closed his eyes and yanked his crane arm free.

Snap! The last support cable broke.

This time, Lofty noticed! His eyes widened as he saw the tree start to sway.

"Timber!" he yelled, warning the team and the Spring City Rockets to move a safe distance away.

Everyone moved, but Lofty was frozen.

"Bob, what do I do?" Lofty asked.

Bob jumped on Lofty's footplate. "Move to your right. Now!" Bob directed him.

Lofty swerved out of harm's way, just before the giant tree fell to the ground with a loud crash. Luckily, no one was hurt, but the display was ruined.

"Oh dear. What a mess!" Bob said. Then he turned to Lofty. "What happened?"

Lofty saw Bob's present underneath the fallen tree and brought it over. "I was trying to give you this present, but I wasn't paying attention. Now I've ruined everything," Lofty said. "I'm sorry, Bob."

Bob opened the box and pulled out a shiny gold star. "My own Christmas decoration, like the ones in the Yard! Thank you, Lofty!"

That gave Lofty an idea. "We can fix the display by covering up the broken parts with snowflake decorations... and we can make them out of ice tiles that broke when the tree fell!"

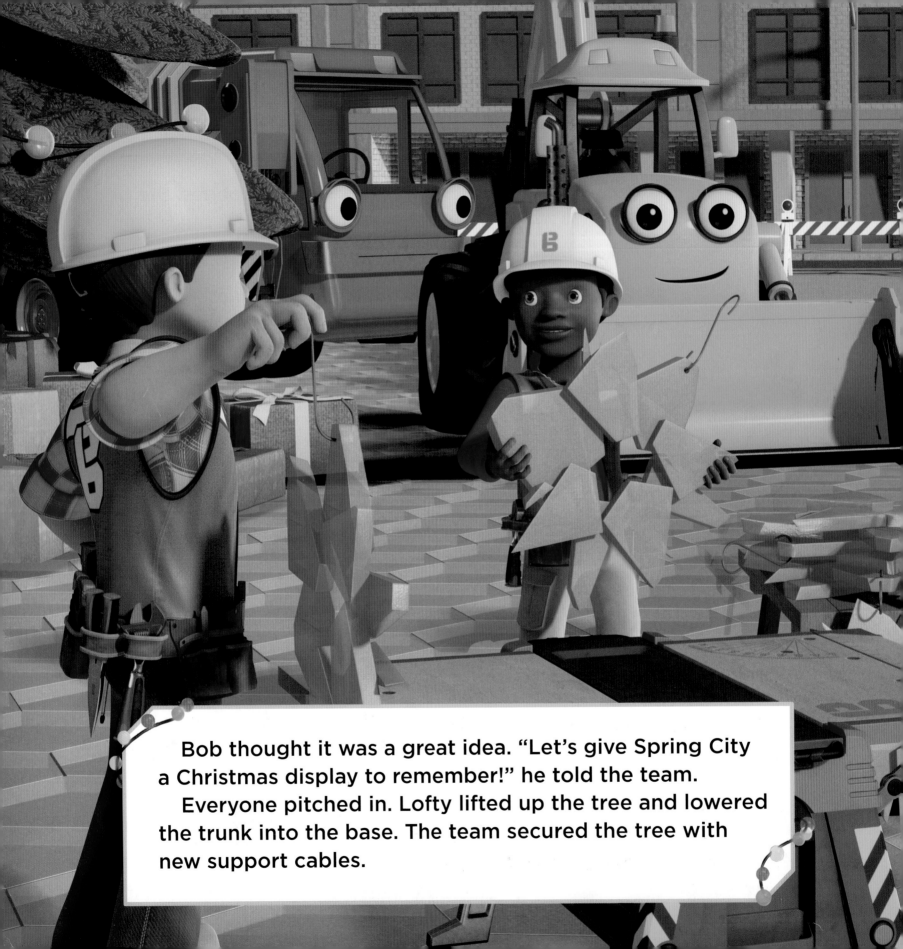

Bob thought it was a great idea. "Let's give Spring City a Christmas display to remember!" he told the team.

Everyone pitched in. Lofty lifted up the tree and lowered the trunk into the base. The team secured the tree with new support cables.

Bob, Wendy, and Leo glued pieces of broken ice tiles together to make giant snowflakes. They drilled a hole in each one and threaded wire through to make hooks. When they hung the new snowflake decorations on the tree, it looked as good as new!

Bob wanted to add *one* more thing: He asked Lofty to put the shiny gold star on top!

The tree looked better than ever...just in time for Mayor Madison to begin the tree-lighting ceremony. Christmas music played as crowds gathered around.

"As your mayor, it gives me great pleasure to turn on Spring City's Christmas display in three, two, one..." Mayor Madison said. She pressed a button on her remote. "Merry Christmas, everyone!"

The tree lights twinkled brightly, and everyone cheered and clapped. Then the snow machines began to whirr.

"Ooh!" Brandon, JJ, Saffi, and Mila gasped as snow fell around the Plaza.

It didn't seem like the Christmas display could get any better.

Then the laser beams turned on! Colorful rays reflected on the ice-tile snowflakes, creating patterns of light on the tree and around the Plaza.

Bob and the team watched proudly.

"Merry Christmas, team!" Bob said. "We did it!"

"Merry Christmas, Bob!" said Wendy, Leo, Muck, Scoop, and Lofty.

It was the most beautiful Christmas display Spring City had ever seen! At the top of the tree, the gold star Lofty gave to Bob sparkled in the light. It was the perfect spot for the perfect Christmas present.

Bob smiled. "Merry Christmas, Lofty!" he said.

Lofty beamed. "Merry Christmas, Bob!"